Little, Brown and Company

Hachette Book Group
237 Park Avenue, New York, NY 10017
Visit our website at lb-kids.com
mylittlepony.com

LB kids is an imprint of Little, Brown and Company.
The LB kids name and logo are trademarks of Hachette Book Group, Inc.

The publisher is not responsible for websites (or their content) that are not owned by the publisher.

First Edition: August 2014

Library of Congress Cataloging-in-Publication Data

Jakobs, D. (Devlan), 1974– author.
 Tricks and treats / adapted by D. Jakobs ; based on the episode by
M. A. Larson. — First edition.
     pages cm. — (My little pony)
 Summary: Twilight Sparkle and her friends dress up in silly costumes for Nightmare Night, but the appearance of Princess Luna terrifies everyone in Ponyville.
  ISBN 978-0-316-24795-5 (pbk)
 1. Ponies—Juvenile fiction. 2. Costume—Juvenile fiction. [1. Ponies—Fiction.
2. Costume—Fiction.] I. Larson, M. A., screenwriter. II. Title. III. Series: My little pony.
  PZ7.J1535545Tr 2014
  [E]—dc23
                                                                                           2013033962

10 9 8 7 6 5 4 3 2

CW

Printed in the United States of America

Licensed By:

My Little Pony: Tricks and Treats

Based on the episode by **M. A. Larson**
Adapted by **D. Jakobs**

LITTLE, BROWN & COMPANY
LB kids

It's Nightmare Night in Ponyville! Everypony has spent months coming up with the very best costume and practicing the Nightmare Night chant: "Nightmare Night! What a fright! Give us something sweet to bite!"

Pipsqueak scampers back to Luna and reaches up to tug on her tail. "Princess Luna? Will you come back next year and scare us again?"

Luna smiles. "We shall have to bring Nightmare Night back!"

Pipsqueak squeals with glee. "Nightmare Night is my favorite night of the year. And you're my favorite princess ever!" He gives her a big hug.

Dear Princess Celestia,

When you first sent me to Ponyville, I didn't know anything about friendship. Today I saw somepony who was having the same problem: your sister, Princess Luna. I'm happy to report that all of Ponyville has learned that even if somepony seems a little intimidating—even scary—when you offer your friendship, you'll discover a whole new pony underneath.

Your faithful student,
Twilight Sparkle

Twilight Sparkle has worked long and hard on her costume, sewing it all by herself. She is dressed as the legendary wizard Star Swirl the Bearded!

But Spike doesn't get it. "Who are you supposed to be?" he asks. "A kooky grandpa?"

Knock-knock-knock! Spike and Twilight open the door to a princess, an astronaut, and a ladybug.

A teeny-tiny pirate is there, too. "Is that you, Pipsqueak?" asks Twilight.

"Sure is! It's my first Nightmare Night ever," Pipsqueak proudly announces.

Suddenly, there is a rustling in the crowd. A chicken pushes in front of the smaller ponies.

"Pinkie Pie? Aren't you a little old for this?" says Twilight Sparkle.

"Too old for free candy?" Pinkie Pie is shocked. "Never!"

Just then, Rainbow Dash floats over their heads on a small, dark cloud. With a sneaky smile, she smashes the cloud with her hooves. Lightning and thunder crash down.

The Pegasus laughs. "Nightmare Night is the best time for pranks."

According to the legend of Nightmare Night, many years ago ponies had to dress up in crazy costumes so Nightmare Moon could not find them. Most ponies in Equestria know that Nightmare Moon has turned back into Princess Luna. But a thousand years of Nightmare Moon is hard to forget!

Everypony gathers in the
town square—and it looks
great! There are games,
like Spider Toss and Apple
Bobbing. The young ponies
clip-clop down the street,
feeling just a little bit scared.
Who's that in the sky?

"Ooh, it's Princess Luna," murmurs Twilight Sparkle.
"It's Nightmare Moon!" yells Pinkie Pie. "Run!"
"What's everypony so scared of?" asks the mayor.
Princess Luna steps out of the shadows, her dark,
starry mane flowing in the night breeze. The ponies
gasp and bow low to the ground.

"CITIZENS OF PONYVILLE!" booms Princess Luna. Her voice is so loud, it hurts their ears and blows back their manes. "LET US CHANGE THIS NIGHTMARE CELEBRATION INTO A BRIGHT FEAST!"

"Did you hear that?" shrieks Pinkie Pie. "Nightmare Moon said she's going to feast on us all!"

The townsponies are terrified. Except for one who knows better.

"Princess Luna," says Twilight.

"Hi, my name is—"

"STAR SWIRL THE BEARDED," booms Princess Luna.

"Finally! Somepony who gets my costume! You're still happy we ponies helped you turn back into yourself, right?" asks Twilight.

"WE COULD NOT BE HAPPIER. IS THAT NOT CLEAR?"

"Well, you kind of sound like you're yelling at me."

"BUT THIS IS THE TRADITIONAL ROYAL CANTERLOT VOICE," booms Princess Luna.

Twilight is blown back by Princess Luna's super-loud voice. "Maybe if you lowered your volume," she says, "you'd get a warmer reception here."

"WE ARE NOT SURE WE CAN," replies Princess Luna.

Twilight brings Princess Luna to the quietest pony she knows. Maybe Fluttershy can teach the princess a thing or two about how to speak without blowing ponies away. But first Twilight needs to get Fluttershy to come out of her house!

"Open up, Fluttershy," insists Twilight. They work on speaking softly.

"How is this?" asks Princess Luna in a totally regular voice.

"You did it!" says Twilight Sparkle.

"Can I go back inside now?" whispers Fluttershy as the princess sweeps her up in a hug.

Just then, Pinkie Pie gallops to the house. "Fluttershy, you have to hide us from Nightmare Moon!" she yells. Then Pinkie sees the princess. "Ahhh! She's stolen Fluttershy's voice so she can gobble her up!"

"It is no use." Princess Luna is feeling lonely and hurt.

But Twilight is not ready to give up. "My friend Applejack is one of the most likable ponies around. I'm sure she'll have some ideas."

They return to the town square to find Applejack. "The princess is looking for a little advice on how to fit in around here," says Twilight.

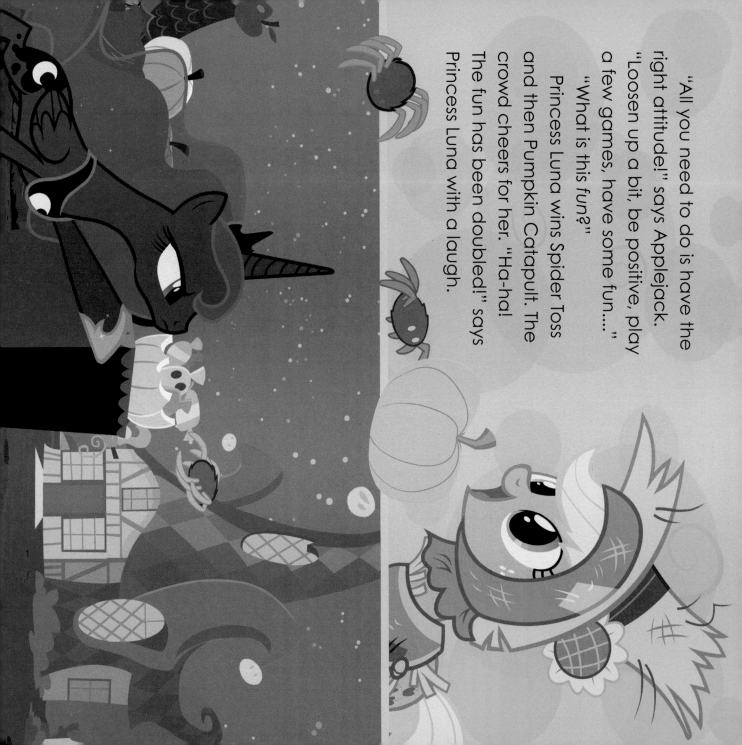

"All you need to do is have the right attitude!" says Applejack.

"Loosen up a bit, be positive, play a few games, have some fun...."

"What is this *fun*?"

Princess Luna wins Spider Toss and then Pumpkin Catapult. The crowd cheers for her. "Ha-ha! The fun has been doubled!" says Princess Luna with a laugh.

"Fair Applejack and villagers," says the princess, "all of you can call me Luna!"

But just then, Luna sees Pipsqueak fall into the apple-bobbing bucket. She dunks her head into the water to rescue him.

"Ahhh! Nightmare Moon is gobbling Pipsqueak!" screams Pinkie Pie. Ponyville is terrified once more.

Luna has had enough. "WE DECREE THAT NIGHTMARE NIGHT SHALL BE CANCELED FOREVER!"

Twilight Sparkle has had enough, too. She lures Pinkie Pie away with a trail of candy. Pinkie Pie can't resist! She pecks up the candy with her beak. Twilight grabs her and covers Pinkie's beak with her hoof.

"No shrieking, no squealing, and no screaming!" says Twilight. "Luna has changed, Pinkie! She doesn't want to gobble you up!"

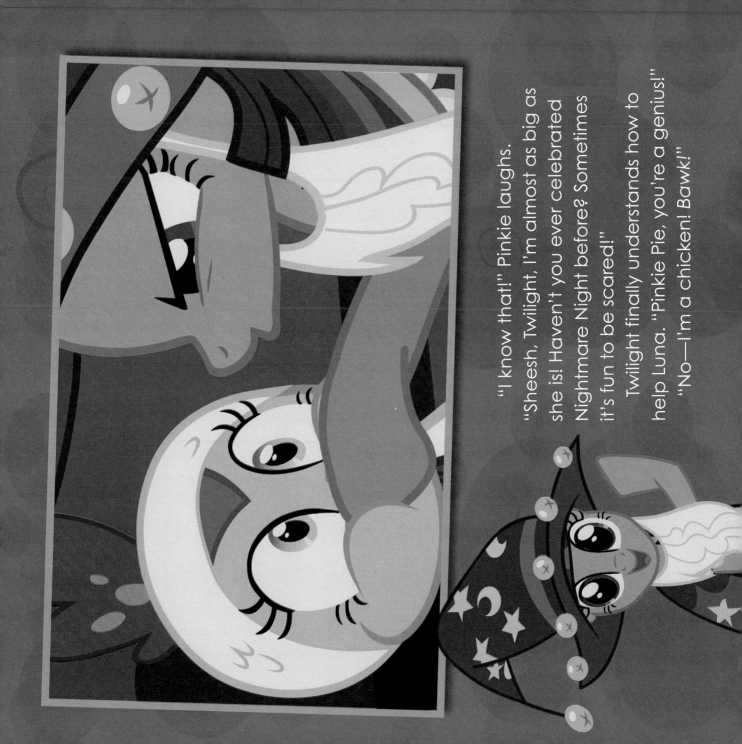

"I know that!" Pinkie laughs.

"Sheesh, Twilight, I'm almost as big as she is! Haven't you ever celebrated Nightmare Night before? Sometimes it's fun to be scared!"

Twilight finally understands how to help Luna. "Pinkie Pie, you're a genius!"

"No—I'm a chicken! *Bawk!*"

Twilight has the mayor lead everypony out to the Nightmare Moon statue. "What's Nightmare Night without the annual candy offering?" she says.

"Good-bye, Nightmare Night. Forever," says Pipsqueak sadly.

But Twilight and Luna are ready for them. "CITIZENS OF PONYVILLE," Luna booms. "I MAY JUST EAT YOUR CANDY—INSTEAD OF YOU!" The ponies scream and run away again.